...ce Blacker has created a splendid character in the magical Ms Wiz. Enormous fun"
The Scotsman

"Sparkling zany humour . . . brilliantly funny"
Children's Books of the Year

TIME FLIES FOR MS WIZ

POWER-CRAZY MS WIZ

MS WIZ LOVES DRACULA

Terence Blacker

Illustrated by Tony Ross

MACMILLAN
CHILDREN'S BOOKS

Time Flies for Ms Wiz
First published 1992 by Piccadilly Press Ltd
Young Piper edition published 1993 by Pan Macmillan Children's Books
This edition published 1997 by Macmillan Children's Books
Power-Crazy Ms Wiz
First published 1992 by Piccadilly Press Ltd
Published 1993 by Pan Macmillan Children's Books
This edition published 1997 by Macmillan Children's Books
Ms Wiz Loves Dracula
First published 1993 by Piccadilly Press Ltd
Published 1994 by Macmillan Children's Books
This edition published 1997 by Macmillan Children's Books

This omnibus edition published 2003 by Macmillan Children's Books
a division of Macmillan Publishers Limited
20 New Wharf Road, London N1 9RR
Basingstoke and Oxford
www.panmacmillan.com

Associated companies throughout the world

ISBN 0 330 42040 2

Text copyright © Terence Blacker 1992, 1993
Illustrations copyright © Tony Ross 1997

The rights of Terence Blacker and Tony Ross to be identified as the
author and illustrator of this work has been asserted by them in accordance
with the Copyright, Designs and Patents Act 1988.

35798642

A CIP catalogue record for this book is available from
the British Library

Phototypeset by Intype London Ltd
Printed and bound in Great Britain by Mackays of Chatham plc, Kent

TIME FLIES FOR MS WIZ

For Lorraine Boyce and the children of
Wyndcliffe Junior School, Birmingham

ACKNOWLEDGEMENTS

I would like to thank Alice Blacker and Classes 3, 4, 5 and 6 at Allfarthing Primary School, Wandsworth, for helping me with ideas used in this story.

CHAPTER ONE

Jack Beddows is History

"King Henry VIII. Sir Walter Raleigh. Ethelred the Unready . . ." Mr Bailey, the teacher of Class Three at St Barnabas School, called out the names as, his chalk squeaking, he wrote them on the blackboard.

"Who are these guys?" muttered Jack, who was sitting at the back of the class. "Who was Ethel and why wasn't she ready?"

"They're historical characters." Mr Bailey turned to the class, his bushy eyebrows sitting up in what Jack thought of as the Mad March Hare position. "And that's your project for the term – to write about your favourite character in history. You can choose anyone you like. Florence Nightingale, Gunga Din—"

Podge put up his hand. "Can I write something on the man who made the most important invention since time began?" he asked.

"Of course," smiled Mr Bailey. "What did he invent?"

"Chocolate," said Podge. "Thick, creamy, chunky— "

"A serious suggestion, please," said Mr Bailey, raising his voice above the laughter.

There was a long silence in the classroom during which the only

sound that could be heard was the
ticking of a clock on the wall. Then,
slowly, a hand was raised at the front
of the class.

"Sir?" It was Nabila Arshad, the
youngest girl in Class Three who had
arrived at St Barnabas that term. "My
choice will be Joan of Arc."

"Who's that?" muttered Jack.
"Noah's wife?"

"She was a young French peasant
girl who lived five hundred years
ago," said Nabila. "One day she heard

voices telling her to lead the French army against the English, so she became a great soldier."

"Weird," said Katrina. "What happened to her?"

"She was burnt at the stake as a witch."

At that moment there was a faint humming noise from outside the classroom. Puzzled, Mr Bailey looked out of the window. As his back was turned, the children saw a sheet of paper appearing out of thin air in front of the blackboard, then floating down on to the desk.

Mr Bailey returned to his desk and picked up the note. "Why did no one tell me this was here?" he asked, walking quickly to the door. "I have to see the Head Teacher," he said. "I want you all to think about your history project until I get back."

It was shortly after Mr Bailey had left the classroom that Caroline noticed an alarm clock on his desk.

"Strange," she said quietly. "I didn't see that before." She stood up and, having looked out of the window to check that Mr Bailey had crossed the playground on his way to the Head's study, she walked up to the desk. "It's a Mickey Mouse alarm clock," she said.

"Go on, set me then," said Mickey.

Caroline leapt back.

"It . . . it spoke!" she gasped.

The rest of the class gathered around the desk.

"Hurry up," said the clock. "Time waits for no woman."

"I know that voice," said Jack. "And it doesn't belong to Mickey Mouse."

He picked up the clock and carefully moved the alarm button around. Suddenly there was a loud ringing, followed by a puff of smoke – and there, standing by the clock, was a woman in bright blue clothes. She had long dark hair and black nail varnish on her fingernails.

"Ms Wiz!" said Jack. "Of course, it had to be you."

Ms Wiz dusted herself down. "Sorry to give you a fright, Class Three," she said. "I heard someone mention the word 'witch' and thought you might be needing a bit of magic."

"You could help us with our history projects for a start," said Jack. "How can I write about my favourite historical character when I don't know any history?"

6

Ms Wiz picked up the Mickey Mouse alarm clock. "It just so happens that I have a brand new spell. With this magic timepiece in one hand and an ordinary calculator in the other, I can travel through time. So who'd like to go back in history for their project?"

"Er, I think I'll stick to the library," said Caroline quickly.

"I get travel sick," said Podge.

"There's something on telly tonight that I don't want to miss," said Katrina.

"What about you, Nabila?" asked Ms Wiz.

All heads turned to where Nabila was still sitting at her desk.

"I'd love to go back in time," she said.

"You'll get stuck there," said Podge. "Ms Wiz's spells always seem to go wrong."

"And what about the time I saved the library?" said Ms Wiz. "And the day Herbert the rat climbed up the school inspector's trousers?"

Class Three were so busy remembering Ms Wiz's spells of the past that nobody noticed Jack picking up the Mickey Mouse clock, wandering back to his desk and reaching for his calculator.

That is, nobody noticed, until the alarm on the clock went off.

"Jack!" Ms Wiz shouted – but it was too late. There was the sound of a loud humming noise, followed by a puff of smoke. The clock and the calculator fell to the floor. As the smoke cleared, Jack was nowhere to be seen.

"Oh dear." Ms Wiz had gone quite pale. "We seem to have lost Jack."

"My best friend," said Podge. "Where is he?"

"He must be somewhere in the last five hundred years," said Ms Wiz, picking up the calculator. "Ah," she smiled with relief. "This shows

the numbers 138, which is what we call The Time-Shift Co-efficient. It means—" she tapped some figures on the calculator "—that Jack's in 1854. Or 138 years before that, which is 1716. Or back another 138 years to 1578. Then if you call The Time-Shift Co-efficient 138x and use simple long division—"

"Never mind simple long division!" Podge seemed on the verge of tears. "How are you going to get Jack back?"

Ms Wiz glanced up to see Mr Bailey crossing the playground on his way back from the Head Teacher's study. "Quick," she said. "I need someone to help me fetch Jack. Where's my time-traveller?"

Nabila stood up.

"Ready when you are," she said quietly.

Ms Wiz jabbed a few numbers on Jack's calculator. "We won't be long, Class Three," she said. "And, while we're gone, the clock will stand still, so we'll literally be back in no time."

"What's she talking about?" muttered Podge.

As the door began to open, Ms Wiz handed the calculator to Nabila. The alarm on the clock sounded.

Mr Bailey stood at the door. "Now who—?"

With a puff of smoke, Ms Wiz and Nabila were gone.

CHAPTER TWO
Queen Who?

Travelling through time is not a
comfortable experience. It's like being
lifted by a great gale and carried
through space at incredible speed
while all you can see before your eyes
is a sort of green minestrone soup.
Then, after thirty seconds, the strange,
deafening hum in your ears starts to
fade as you fall down and down
towards the year of your choice to
land with a bump.

"Ouch," said Nabila. "My bum."

"Honestly," said a voice behind her.
"I take you back four hundred years
in time and all you can say is 'Ouch,
my bum.' "

"Ms Wiz?" Nabila turned to see a
young woman in a brown peasant
smock, sitting on the grass beside her.

"You look good," smiled Ms Wiz.

Nabila realised that she too was dressed like a peasant girl. "Four hundred years," she said quietly. "So we have to be in the clothes of the period."

"Jeans would get us noticed," said Ms Wiz, getting to her feet. "Come on, we had better start looking for Jack."

"How do we know he's here?" asked Nabila, following her towards a group of thatched cottages that were nearby. "He could be anywhere in the world."

"If you use the same calculator, you always land in the same place. It's a basic rule of time-travel. By the way, you'll find the calculator in your pocket. Don't lose it or we'll be stuck in 1578 for the rest of our lives."

For the first time, Nabila began to feel nervous. "My mum and dad will be worried about me."

"No they won't," said Ms Wiz. "When we get back to St Barnabas, it will be as if we had only been gone a

few minutes. We've stepped out of
time."

"Does that mean we don't exist?"

Ms Wiz stopped. "Yikes, maybe
it does," she said, frowning. "You
know your trouble, Nabila? You
think too much."

"At school, they call me Nabby
Know-all. Just because I prefer
reading books to running around
after a ball."

"I know," said Ms Wiz.

Nabila looked at her curiously.

"What – that the children think I'm
odd because I'm so quiet?"

Ms Wiz nodded.

"That—" Nabila looked away,
"—that I haven't got any real friends
at St Barnabas?"

"But what would happen if
you rescued Jack?" said Ms Wiz.
"What if you brought him back to
the present when all the other
children of Class Three had been
nervous about a bit of time-
travel?"

"I suppose they'd notice me then," said Nabila. "We're not going to get stuck here, are we?"

"And another reason I chose you," said Ms Wiz quickly, ignoring Nabila's question, "is that you can tell me what to expect. For example, what's happening now in 1578?"

"Well, Queen Elizabeth I was on the throne and—"

"Queen Who?" Ms Wiz saw the look of astonishment on Nabila's face. "I'm sorry but at the school I went to, Paranormal Operatives Comprehensive, they only taught things like Spell Technology, Advanced Potion-Making and Practical Magic. We didn't have time for history."

"Actually, I don't know much about Elizabeth," said Nabila. "Except she was very powerful, wore a wig of reddish hair and used to go round saying things like, 'I may have the body of a weak and feeble woman but I have the heart and stomach of a king.' "

"Weak and feeble woman?" Ms Wiz looked shocked. "I don't like that at all."

"It was a long time ago," said Nabila.

As they approached the village, they could see some children chasing a dog that was barking and wagging its tail. A boy of about ten, who had been playing with the other children, looked up and came running towards them.

"Ducking, ducking," he shouted. "Strangers are here for the ducking."

Soon the other children had gathered around. A tall girl with mud in her matted blonde hair touched Nabila's hand. "Why are you so brown?" she asked.

"My parents came from Pakistan," said Nabila.

"Pakistan?" The girl frowned. "That is a funny sounding village."

"Yes, it's just a few miles away," said Ms Wiz quickly. "The sun shines all the year round." She dropped her voice. "I'm going into the village," she said. "You stay here with the children. Ask them if they've seen any children who look like Jack."

"But Ms Wiz—"

"I have to look for someone in the village," said Ms Wiz, turning to the children. "Can Nabila stay with you for a few minutes?"

"Nabila? What a pretty name," said the tall girl. She took Nabila's hand. "I'm Molly. Can you play hopscotch?"

For the ten minutes she was playing with the children, Nabila almost forgot that they were living over four hundred years before she was born. They were just as rough and rowdy as the children of St Barnabas.

"I need to rest," she said eventually.

Molly laughed. "Don't they play

hopscotch in your village?"

"To tell the truth, I prefer reading."

"Reading?" Molly looked puzzled. "What's that then?"

Nabila shook her head. "Never mind," she said. "I suppose you haven't seen a stranger in the village, have you? He's called Jack."

"There are a couple of Jacks in the village but I've known them since I was small. Is this friend from Pakistan too?"

"No, er – well, near to Pakistan."

"So he'll be brown-skinned too."

"No." Nabila smiled. "He stays indoors a lot."

As they spoke, the sound of voices could be heard coming from the village.

"Come on, then." Molly leapt to her feet. "It's starting."

They followed the other children down a path between the houses, where chickens, pigs and geese wandered free. As they turned into a main street, Nabila saw, gathered in front of the village pond, a crowd of about a hundred people, laughing and jeering. It was only when she and Molly had pushed their way to the front that Nabila saw the reason for their laughter.

A girl of about sixteen was strapped to a chair on the end of a plank, poised over the pond. Through her wild dark hair, her eyes were wide with terror.

"That poor girl," said Nabila. "What are they doing to her?"

"She's no girl," said Molly. "She's P-Peg the Witch. Got the devil in her."

"She doesn't look like a witch to me."

"If you heard her talk, you'd know." Molly laughed. "M-m-my n-n-name's P-Peg. Devil talk."

"She's got a stutter," said Nabila desperately. "It's not her fault."

The cheers grew louder as four of the village men prepared to release the end of the plank that was on dry land. "Duck her!" the villagers were shouting. "Duck the witch!"

At first, Nabila thought that the faint humming sound she heard was in her imagination. Then she could hear the sound of a horse's hooves approaching from the far end of the village. A woman, wearing a small crown on her flaming red hair, was approaching on a magnificent white horse.

There was a gasp from the villagers as they saw the woman. "The queen," they whispered to one another. "It's Her Majesty!"

The woman raised her left hand and the crowd fell silent.

"My subjects," she cried. "I may have the body of a weak and—" she hesitated.

Nabila smiled as she saw who it was. "The body of a weak and feeble woman, Ms Wiz," she

whispered under her breath.

"—the body of a weak and fantastically intelligent woman," cried Ms Wiz. "But I have the heart and stomach of a . . . queen!"

There was a gasp from the crowd. "Your Majesty, you honour us with your presence," said a fat, red-faced man, falling to his knees before the white horse.

"Release this girl!" said Ms Wiz. "By order of Queen Elizabeth I."

With quick, panicky gestures, the four men pulled in the plank and untied the girl.

"Come here, my child," Ms Wiz said more gently.

The crowd parted as the girl they had called P-Peg the Witch made her way forward to stand in front of Ms Wiz on her horse.

"If you touch her again, you will be executed. Understand?"

There were murmurs of nervous agreement from the crowd.

"Don't go too far, Ms Wiz," muttered Nabila under her breath.

"Anyway, she isn't a witch," said Ms Wiz on her horse. "She's just got a minor speech deficiency."

"What's she saying?" asked a man near the front. "Sounds like strange talk coming from a queen."

Ms Wiz held up a hand majestically. "Is there a girl called Nabila in this village?" she asked.

Her heart thumping, Nabila made

her way forward until she stood beside Peg.

"My child," said Ms Wiz. "Give me the article you have in your smock."

As Nabila fumbled in her pocket for the calculator, she was aware that the crowd were growing restless around her.

"If she's the queen, where are her soldiers?" the fat man asked loudly.

"Here, that queen's got black fingernails," said a woman standing nearby.

"Let's get out of here," Ms Wiz whispered urgently, taking the clock from her pocket. "I've never ridden a horse before in my life."

"But what about Peg?" Nabila asked. "We can't just leave her."

"Hold her hand!" said Ms Wiz.

As the murmurings from the villagers grew louder, Peg backed away from Nabila in fear. "N-n-n-no," she said.

Nabila saw that Ms Wiz was

already pressing some numbers on the calculator. With a desperate lunge, she grabbed Peg's smock and, with the other hand, reached for Ms Wiz's outstretched hand.

"Now, Ms Wiz!" she shouted. "Now!"

CHAPTER THREE

Russskies in Breeches

It was the noise that Nabila noticed
first. Men shouting, the neighing of
frightened horses, some strange
distant booms. Slowly she opened
her eyes – then snapped them shut.

"Er, no, Ms Wiz," she said quickly,
"I don't think we'll stay here. You
seem to have landed us in the middle
of a war."

Ms Wiz stood up and touched her
silver wig. "It's 1854. I wasn't to
know that there was a war going on
then."

"Hit the calculator!" wailed Nabila.
"If I die in a war that took place a
hundred years before I was born, my
parents will kill me!"

"Nonsense," said Ms Wiz, brushing
down her pink crinoline dress. "This
is just the sort of place we'll find Jack.

That boy seems to attract trouble."

It was now that Nabila looked more closely at Ms Wiz. In spite of her fear, she started laughing.

"This is serious," said Ms Wiz. "War's no joking matter, you know."

"Our clothes," said Nabila, looking at the large golden fan that she was carrying. "People weren't wearing powdered wigs and huge, silly skirts in 1854. We're a hundred years out of date."

Ms Wiz frowned. "Weren't they? I'm sure that I did the right spell."

"Beautiful," said a voice behind them. Nabila turned to see Peg, staring in wonderment at the sky-blue and silver gown she was wearing. "I don't understand," she said in a soft brogue. "What happened?"

"Her stutter," said Nabila. "It's gone."

"Yes." Ms Wiz was fiddling with the Mickey Mouse alarm clock. "Time-travel does that sometimes – it's the shock." There was a faint humming noise, a flash – and Nabila found that she was back in her normal clothes. Ms Wiz and Peg were dressed in T-shirts and jeans.

"That's more comfortable," smiled Ms Wiz.

"We don't exactly look as if we came from 1854," said Nabila.

"Halt!" They heard the sound of cantering hooves behind them as a soldier approached. "Who goes there?" he cried, reining in his horse.

"Only us," said Ms Wiz with a smile. "The thing is, we're looking for a boy called Jack Beddows. He was messing around with my time machine over one hundred and thirty years from now and suddenly – you are listening, aren't you?"

"Ladies?" The man stroked his moustache suspiciously. "Ladies in breeches and odd coloured shirts?"

"Yes, yes." Ms Wiz smiled. "That's what you'll be wearing in the future. At least not you because you won't be around but—"

"*Spies*!" the man shouted suddenly. "Help! Russian spies are upon us! Dressed as ladies in breeches!" He pulled a sword from the scabbard on his belt. "Russkies," he said, pointing the blade at Ms Wiz's throat. "You're under arrest."

"Is this a dream I'm having?" Peg whispered.

Nabila sighed. "I wish it were," she said.

A few minutes later, Ms Wiz, Nabila and Peg were led into a dark, velvet-lined tent. There, seated behind a huge desk on which there was a map, was an older man. In one hand he held a glass of red wine and in the other was a cigar.

"Lord Cardigan, sir!" barked the soldier who had captured them. "I found these three wandering through the camp. They admit to being Russian spies."

"We never!" Nabila burst out. "We just said—"

"Silence!" shouted the soldier.

"Russians?" Lord Cardigan put a monocle to his right eye and peered. "You-ov speak-ov English-ov?"

Ms Wiz sighed. "Your lordship, there has been a terrible misunderstanding." She smiled. "It's

all very simple. We are time-travellers searching for a friend of ours who, we believe, might have landed in 1854."

She took the Mickey Mouse alarm clock out of a bag she was carrying. "Look, this is our time machine."

Lord Cardigan took the clock. "Oh yes," he said, smiling like a little boy who has been given a present. "There's a funny mousey on the front. It's an *excellent* time machine. Thank you very much."

"Careful, sir," said the soldier standing beside them. "It might be a trick."

"It's not a present," said Ms Wiz. "We don't want you zooming through time too, do we?"

Lord Cardigan held on to the clock with both hands. "Mine now," he said.

"Well done, Ms Wiz," muttered Nabila.

"What about you two?" Lord Cardigan turned suddenly to Nabila and Peg. "Are you Russian spies too?" he asked. "Where do you come from?"

"I'm from Class Three at St Barnabas School," said Nabila.

"And I'm a village girl from the reign of Queen Elizabeth I, who's having a very odd dream," said Peg.

Before Lord Cardigan could say anything, another soldier burst into the tent.

"The Russians are about to capture our guns at the end of the valley, sir," he said. "Lord Raglan says we should attack."

"Right!" Lord Cardigan leapt to his feet. "Call up the Light Brigade. We're going to charge."

"No!" Nabila said quickly. "Now I remember what happened in 1854. It was called the Charge of the Light Brigade – you go up the wrong valley and it's all a terrible mistake. I saw a film about it."

"Film? What in deuce's name is a film?"

"You see, sir?" The first soldier barked. "Russian spies, sir. Trying to stop the attack, sir. Given themselves away, sir."

"Quite right." Lord Cardigan was rolling up the map. "Lock them up until we've finished our charge."

"Could we just have our clock back?" said Ms Wiz.

"Funny mousey?" Lord Cardigan looked shocked. "No, he's a prisoner too, aren't you, mousey? Take them away!"

"I think I'd like to wake up now, please," said Peg.

CHAPTER FOUR

The well scared Soldier

Nabila stared into the blackness that
was all around her.

"You could have taken us
anywhere in history," she sighed.
"We could have gone to America
just after it was discovered by
Christopher Columbus. I could have
seen what Pakistan was like in the
time of my great-grandparents. But
where do we go? To the Crimean War
at the Charge of the Light Brigade –
which was a disastrous defeat, by the
way."

The only sound that came from the
darkness was of Peg, sobbing quietly.

"Not that we'll see it since we're
stuck here in a prison tent," Nabila
continued.

"You don't exactly look on the
bright side, do you?" said Ms Wiz at

last. "It wasn't my fault that Jack decided to play with my clock."

"He's probably in the Valley of Death by now," said Nabila, gloomily. "You know that poem 'Into the Valley of Death rode the Six Hundred'? It's the Six Hundred and One now. Poor old Jack."

A light flared in front of Ms Wiz, illuminating her face.

"Magic!" Peg gasped.

"Not really," said Ms Wiz. "I brought an electric torch with me." Before Peg could ask what an electric torch was, Ms Wiz added, "Now *this* is magic."

For about a second, the tent was filled with a humming noise. Then Nabila felt as if a great hand had slapped her on the back. When she opened her eyes, she found she was looking at Peg's foot.

'What's happened?" she asked in a voice that was hers, yet more melodic, like that of—

"A bird!" exclaimed Peg. "Nabila had been turned into a little bird."

"Don't worry, Peg," said Ms Wiz. "She'll be Nabila again soon. Disguised as a little bird, she can search the camp for Jack, then bring him back here and rescue us."

"Why me?" said Nabila weakly in her funny bird voice.

Ms Wiz shrugged. "I really wish I could come with you," she said, "but we can't leave Peg alone."

Carefully, she pushed Nabila under the skirt of the tent. "Hurry back," she whispered.

The sunlight blinded Nabila for an instant. Then, seeing two guards at the entrance to the tent, she took a deep breath, spread her wings and began to fly.

Circling high above the encampment, Nabila could see row upon row of English soldiers on their horses, preparing for the Charge of the Light Brigade, but it wasn't at all like the film she had seen. The men looked tired and dirty as they sat on their thin, mudspattered horses. There was no gleam or sparkle to their uniforms. An atmosphere of fear and weariness hung over the hillside.

"Those poor men," thought Nabila as she looked down. "If only I could warn them," she said to herself.

But she couldn't. Ms Wiz had told her that it was a basic rule of time-travel that you're not allowed to change the course of history.

Near one of the tents, she could see a bird coop, on top of which were sitting three pigeons. Flying down, she noticed that the birds had rings on their legs – they were messenger pigeons, used to take notes from one part of the army to the other.

"Any pigeon round here speak English?" said Nabila, hopping onto the ledge beside the pigeons, whose eyes were half-closed. "Any pigeon round here speak anything?"

"Coo," said one of the pigeons.

"Very helpful, I must say," twittered Nabila.

At that moment, she heard from behind a tent, the sound of a man shouting.

"Can't ride? Call yourself a member of the Light Brigade and you can't even ride? Get on that horse at once, you horrible little man – *now*!"

Nabila flew on to one of the guy ropes – and almost fell off with surprise when she saw what was happening beyond the tent.

There, in full uniform but cowering before the biggest horse she had ever seen, was Jack.

"I c-c-can't ride, sergeant," he was saying to a soldier. "I'm well scared of horses."

"Well scared? Well scared?" The man's face was deep scarlet with rage. "What does well scared mean?"

Nabila decided that it was time for action. "It means he won't be going with you," she said as she flew onto the ground near the soldier.

"What?" The soldier whirled around. It took a moment for him to realise that it was a small sparrow that had been speaking to him.

"You're not imagining it," said Nabila, hopping towards him. "I was a perfectly normal person until I was turned into a bird because I used to shout at people all the time like you're doing. You want to watch out it doesn't happen to you."

The soldier was backing away. "Must be war fever," he muttered to himself. "A bird's talking to me. I'm going mad." He turned and ran in the direction of the other soldiers.

Nabila hopped towards Jack. "If you knew the trouble you've caused us," she said. "We've been looking for you for hundreds of years."

Jack was smiling with relief. "Ms Wiz?"

"Honestly," said the bird. "Do I look like Ms Wiz? I'm Nabila."

"Nabila?"

"Yes, it's Nabby Know-all to the rescue. Now, are you going to follow me or not?"

Jack ran after Nabila as she flew ahead towards the prison tent.

"You keep the guards busy, while I sneak into the tent," said Nabila.

Jack walked up to the two soldiers who were standing at the entrance to the tent. "Is it visiting hour for the prisoners yet?" he asked.

"Visiting hour? What are you talking about?" said the taller of the two guards.

"Hop it, soldier," said the second. "Or we'll—"

He looked around him as a faint humming sound filled the air. Suddenly the guards were enveloped in a puff of smoke. When it cleared, they were standing in white silk leggings, buckled shoes and wigs.

"That is my clothes spell," said a voice coming from the tent behind them. *If you don't leave us, I'll make sure that you go into the Charge of the Light Brigade stark naked.*"

"Wh-what?" said the first soldier, nervously glancing over his shoulder. The other took the wig off his head and looked at it in amazement. "Let's get out of here," he said.

As the guards hurried off, Ms Wiz and Peg emerged from the tent.

"Well done, Nabila," said Ms Wiz to the little sparrow who was perched on her shoulder.

"Hullo," said Jack to Peg. "Where did you come from?"

"It's a long story," said Nabila. "We'll tell you when you get home."

"Why don't we just stay for the battle?" asked Ms Wiz.

"No," said Nabila, a hint of panic in her little bird voice. "I hate violence."

"All right," said Ms Wiz, taking the calculator from the back pocket of her jeans. "Now where did I leave that clock?"

It was Lord Cardigan's proudest moment. He trotted past line after line of his troops as they waited for the order to advance into the valley below. He was thinking of his name in the history books of

the future – the general who commanded the great Charge of the Light Brigade.

Behind his saddle was strapped his newest toy, a timepiece showing the face of a big-eared mouse. Perhaps, he thought to himself, it would bring him luck.

Lord Cardigan was so absorbed in his thoughts that he ignored the humming noise coming from the camp behind him but his horse shied as if something had touched it. When he felt behind his saddle, the clock had gone.

"Mousey?" he said. "Where's funny mousey gone?"

"Light Brigade ready for action, sir," one of his officers called out to him.

At that moment, there was a puff of smoke from in front of the prison tent but Lord Cardigan was too busy spurring his horse forward to notice.

"Charge!" he cried.

CHAPTER FIVE

Just in Time

"—Now who was the joker who sent
me to the Head Teacher's office when
he wasn't even—?" Mr Bailey stood in
the doorway to the classroom, then
frowned. At the front of the class, two
strangers were standing beside Jack.

"Allow me to introduce myself,"
said Ms Wiz, stepping forward and
shaking Mr Bailey by the hand. "My
name's Ms Wiz."

Mr Bailey pulled back his hand as if
he had been given an electric shock.
"The one with the magic rat? The
one who's banned from school for
turning a class into pigeons? The one
who's always causing trouble round
here?"

"Trouble?" Ms Wiz frowned. "I just
liven things up a little bit."

"Dare I ask—" Mr Bailey nodded in

the direction of Peg "—who she is?"

"This is my friend, Peg," said Ms Wiz. "She's a bit shocked because she's just travelled four hundred years through time."

"Four hundred years?" Mr Bailey's eyebrows moved into the rare Frightened Pheasants position. "What exactly is going on here?"

"It's all very simple," said Ms Wiz. "Jack got lost in history, so, while you were frozen in time, Nabila and I had to go back to fetch him. We met Peg who was having a bit of a problem back in 1578, then we went to the Crimean War and – oh *no*!"

At that instant, the very same question occurred to everyone in the classroom.

"Where's Nabila?" asked Caroline.

"Ah, problem," said Ms Wiz. "When we left 1854, she wasn't touching me when I made the spell. Still, she should be somewhere nearby."

"Come on, Ms Wiz," said Jack desperately. "It was Nabila who saved me from the Charge of the Light Brigade."

"She was a bird," said Peg quietly.

"Right, that's it," said Mr Bailey firmly. "I'm going to ring the police to tell them a child's been turned into a bird and has gone missing somewhere in the nineteenth century."

"There are some birds in the playground," said Katrina who had been staring out of the window as usual. "The sparrows all seem to be chasing a little bird that's smaller than the rest of them."

"*Do* something, Ms Wiz!" Jack shouted. "That's Nabila and she's getting scragged by a bunch of sparrows!"

Ms Wiz stood by the window. As she stretched out her arms the familiar humming noise filled the classroom. Suddenly, there was

Nabila sitting in the playground. A
group of birds that were nearby flew
away. She stood up, looked around
her, and smiled with relief.

As Nabila walked back into the
classroom, the children of Class
Three applauded.

"Looks like you're the most
popular girl in class today," laughed
Ms Wiz.

"Silence!" Mr Bailey banged his
desk. "It's all very well travelling

through time," he said, "but perhaps Ms Clever Dick Wiz could answer me this question. If she's so magic, why didn't she stop the Charge of the Light Brigade happening?"

"Imagine there was a Private Smith who was killed in the Charge of the Light Brigade," said Ms Wiz. "Imagine that, because magic stopped it happening, he didn't die but came home to marry a young girl from Lambeth. Except the young girl was meant to marry your great-great-grandfather."

"In other words, the whole of history would have been changed and you wouldn't have been born, Mr Bailey," said Nabila.

"Er, really?" Mr Bailey seemed to be trying to work it out in his head.

"Which would have been *really* sad for Class Three," said Podge innocently.

"Right, history project," said Mr Bailey, changing the subject quickly.

"Who's decided on the character they'll be studying?"

"I'm going to read about Lord Cardigan," said Nabila. "I want to know more about the Charge of the Light Brigade."

Ms Wiz stepped forward. "Since she's here, perhaps Peg could tell you all about village life in 1578," she said.

"Yeah, brilliant," said Jack. "Peg could be our favourite historical character. She could tell us all about herself in her own words."

So, for the next ten minutes, Peg talked in a shy voice about her parents, her job as a shepherdess, how it came about that the villagers thought she was a witch because she had a stammer and about the day she was rescued by Ms Wiz and Nabila.

When the bell rang for the end of the lesson, Mr Bailey stood up. "Very interesting, Peg," he said. "Perhaps it's time for Ms Wiz to take you back

to your village." He looked to the back of the class where Ms Wiz had been sitting and sighed. "*Now* where's that woman gone?"

"Look!" Podge pointed at the blackboard. As if an invisible hand was holding it, a piece of chalk was writing a message on the board. It read:

"HOW TIME FLIES WHEN YOU'RE HAVING FUN! GOOD LUCK, PEG. GOODBYE, CLASS

THREE – I'LL SEE YOU THE NEXT
TIME A BIT OF MAGIC'S
NEEDED . . ."

"If Ms Wiz has gone," said Jack,
"who's going to get Peg back to her
village?"

"Perhaps she'd like to stay," said
Caroline.

"And how am I going to explain
her to the Head Teacher!" asked Mr
Bailey. "Sorry, sir, but I've got a
sixteen-year-old girl from
Elizabethan times in my class?"

"I want to go home," said Peg.

Nabila took her by the hand to Mr
Bailey's desk. There, side by side,
were Jack's calculator and the Mickey
Mouse alarm clock. Carefully she
placed Peg's left hand on the clock.
Then she set the calculator to 1578.

"Bye, Peg, take care," she smiled.

"Thank you, Nabila," said Peg.

As her right hand touched the
calculator, there was a humming
sound, then a puff of smoke. The

calculator fell to the ground as Peg
and the alarm clock disappeared.

"Wow!" said Lizzie. "Nabila's got
magic powers."

"No, that was Ms Wiz magic in the
clock," said Nabila.

"Break time, children," Mr Bailey
called out.

"Of course," said Jack, "school's a
bit boring after you've ridden a huge
charger into battle against thousands
and thousands of Russians—"

"You were a soldier?" gasped
Podge.

It was at that moment that Jack noticed Nabila smiling at him.

"Go on, Jack, this is interesting," she said.

"Well . . . I wasn't exactly *in* the battle," he said. "Maybe Nabila should tell you what really happened."

And the children of Class Three clustered around Nabila as, laughing and asking her questions, they made their way out to the playground.

POWER-CRAZY
MS WIZ

Acknowledgement

I would like to thank the children of Class 12D, Riverside Primary School, Wallasey, whose idea Ms Wiz PM was the inspiration for this story.

CHAPTER ONE

A Lean, Mean Peter Harris

It was the first day of the holidays, the fair was in town and the sun shone high in the sky. But for Peter Harris, better known as Podge, it felt like the worst day of his life.

He wandered through the fairground, thinking of the bad news he had received that morning. The Big Dipper loomed up in front of him but he walked on. He heard the screams and laughter of children on the Waltza – he hardly looked at them. Even the candy floss store, which was normally Podge's first stop at the fair, didn't interest him today.

Deep in thought, he found himself standing in front of a small, circular store decked out with plastic toys and goldfish in transparent plastic bags. There was a table in the middle with some wooden

cubes on it. A sign on the stall read "GET
THE HOOP OVER THE CUBE – TAKE A
GOLDFISH HOME!"

"Want a go, son?" The stallholder, a
red-faced man whose large stomach
stretched his dirty white shirt, held out a
hoop.

Podge shook his head. He never won
anything. Anyway, he wasn't in the
mood.

He was just about to move away when

he noticed that one of the fishes seemed to be looking at him with that wide-eyed help-me expression that Podge's friend Henry Wilson put on when there was a maths test at school. Podge frowned – he didn't want to think of school right now.

"Yes, we'll have a go, please."

Podge turned to see, standing beside him, a girl in torn jeans and a baseball cap. The stallholder gave her a hoop which she passed to Podge.

"No, thanks," said Podge quietly. "I'm useless at throwing things."

"Not today you aren't," said the girl.

Sighing, Podge held the hoop before him and took aim. As he drew his hand back, he was aware of a humming sound all around him. Now where had he heard that before? Concentrating as hard as he could, he let the hoop go.

It moved through the air slowly, like a tiny spacecraft, and hovered over the block, before settling neatly around it.

"Eh?" The stallholder looked at the hoop suspiciously.

"Brilliant throw!" said the girl. "We'll have this goldfish, please." She pointed to the fish which Podge had noticed.

Podge looked at her more closely. She was a bit older than he had thought at first and there was something familiar about her flashing green eyes. "Haven't we met somewhere?" Podge asked.

Without a word, she held up her hand.

On her nails was black nail-varnish.

"Ms Wiz!" Podge smiled for the first time that day. "What are you doing here?"

"You know how it is," said Ms Wiz quietly. "I go wherever magic is needed."

Grumpily, the stallholder handed her the goldfish. "Magic," he muttered. "Looked like good old-fashioned cheating to me."

Ms Wiz put her arm around Podge's shoulders. "So," she said. "Tell me your problem."

"I thought you knew everything," said Podge, turning away from the stall. Ms Wiz followed, holding the goldfish in front of her.

"Not everything," she said. "The message I received this morning was 'MAGIC ALERT – PODGE HARRIS – PARENT PROBLEM'."

"*Major* parent problem," said Podge gloomily. "I'm not sure I really want to talk about it."

Ms Wiz walked into a video arcade

and stood in front of a computer game. "When did the problem take place?" she asked.

"This morning at breakfast."

"And your address is . . . ?"

"15 Rylett Road."

Ms Wiz pressed a few buttons on the machine. Briefly the screen went fuzzy and made a quiet humming sound. Then it cleared to show a modern kitchen. In the centre of the room was a table on either side of which sat a man and a woman, looking very serious. Between them was a child, eating.

"Hey, that's me!" Podge gasped. "That's my kitchen! And there's Mum and Dad!"

"It's a magical reconstruction of your kitchen at breakfast this morning. It's going to show me what happened."

"Oh no." Podge winced. "This is going to be really embarrassing."

*

On the screen, the figures started talking.

"Now Peter, we need to have a serious discussion," Podge's father, Mr Harris, was saying.

"Voff avout?" said Podge.

"*Don't* talk with your mouth full," Mr Harris snapped.

"Podge swallowed. "Sorry," he said.

"Today's the start of your holidays, Peter," his father continued. "And from now on there are going to be some changes around here."

"Changes?"

"Number one, you're going to spend less time with your nose in a book, reading stories, and more time learning for exams."

"But—"

"Number two, you're going on a diet. You look like a football on legs. So it's no more chocolate biscuits. This time next month I want to see a lean, mean Peter Harris."

"Lean? Mean?"

"Number three." Mr Harris paused. "I'm taking you away from that school of yours."

Podge gasped.

"St Barnabas." Mr Harris spat the words out in disgust. "All you get there is . . . larking about."

"What about my friends?" Podge protested.

"There'll be time enough for friends when you've passed a few exams," said Mr Harris, getting to his feet. "My decision's final and I won't budge. Will I, Mother?"

"No," Mrs Harris had sighed wearily. "You won't budge."

"Hmm, I see the problem now," said Ms Wiz, as the images faded from the screen. "Somehow we've got to make your father change his mind."

"Some hope," Podge muttered. "You'd

have to be Prime Minister to make my dad change his mind."

"Hey, great vid!" said a voice behind them. Ms Wiz and Podge turned to see Jack Beddows, Podge's best friend. "What did you have to do to win?" said Jack, looking at the screen. "Get the big boy through the kitchen door?"

"Great joke," said Podge.

"I saw you with Ms Wiz," said Jack. "I thought you were playing a game."

"That was no game," said Ms Wiz. "It was real – Podge is being taken away from St Barnabas. It's time for action." She walked out of the video arcade in the direction of the dodgem cars.

"I don't believe it," Jack said to Podge.

"And I'm being put on a diet," said Podge. "My dad says I look like a football on legs. That's not true, is it?"

"Er, well—"

Fortunately for Jack, they were interrupted by Ms Wiz waving to them from a purple dodgem car. "Come on," she shouted. "We've got no time to lose."

"Typical Ms Wiz," said Podge. "It's the most serious day of my life and she wants to ride a bumper car."

Both of them squeezed into the dodgem, with Podge in the driving seat.

"I say." A man eating some candy floss nearby pointed to the dodgem car. "You're only allowed two people per car, you know. I think one of you really ought to get out."

"Do you?" said Ms Wiz innocently.

As the man walked towards a fairground assistant, the candy floss he was holding seemed to be growing larger and larger until, seconds later, it covered the whole of his head and the top of his body.

"Help!" he shouted in a muffled voice. "Where am I? Everything's gone pink."

"Let's go," said Ms Wiz. She reached under her seat and took out a white umbrella which she fixed to the front of the dodgem. It began to turn, faster and faster, like the propeller of a helicopter.

"Er, no, Ms Wiz," said Podge nervously as the dodgem floated upwards. "I don't think this is one of your better ideas."

But the dodgem seemed to have a life of its own. It climbed higher and higher over the fairground.

"Brilliant ride," said Jack. "And we didn't even pay."

"I hate heights!" Podge was clinging on to the steering wheel. "I get travel-sick. This is meant to be a bumper car, not a bumper plane."

As the dodgem picked up speed, Ms Wiz took off her baseball cap and let the wind blow through her long, dark hair. "London, here we come."

"Why are we going to London?" Jack asked.

"Didn't I tell you?" Ms Wiz raised her voice above the whistling of the wind.

"We're off to see the Prime Minister. It was Podge's idea."

"*What?*" said Podge. "I never—"

"Well done, Podge," shouted Jack.

CHAPTER TWO

Mad Goldfish Disease

A purple dodgem car, suspended by a whirling white umbrella, flew high over the streets of London.

As it skimmed a few feet above Buckingham Palace, it seemed to be slowing down.

"Now here's what we're going to do," said Ms Wiz to Podge and Jack. "In a few moments' time, we shall be meeting the Prime Minister—"

"Yeah yeah," muttered Jack who didn't believe anything until he could see it.

"—and I shall be asking him to pass a new law to prevent parents taking children away from schools against their wishes."

"Are you sure he can pass laws all by himself?" asked Podge.

"Of course he can," said Ms Wiz. "He's Prime Minister, isn't he?"

"I think it may be a bit more complicated than that," said Jack.

"Honestly, you two!" Ms Wiz crossed her arms, almost crushing the goldfish she was carrying. "You're so . . . negative. Just trust me."

"We'll have to," said Jack, looking over the edge of the dodgem. "We're coming in to land."

"Now it's very important that we act as a team," said Ms Wiz. "I'll be in charge, Podge will be my adviser and Jack will look after Henry?"

"Henry?"

"Named after Henry Wilson at school," said Podge.

Ms Wiz passed Jack the bag containing the goldfish. "This is Henry," she smiled. "He's very important."

"Typical," grumbled Jack. "Ms Wiz gets the power, Podge gets the fun and I get the goldfish."

The dodgem hovered a few feet above a wide pavement. As it landed, a small crowd of people gathered on the pavement, staring and pointing.

A tall, bearded policeman pushed his way towards them. Taking one look at the dodgem, he reached into his top pocket for a notebook. "No number plates," he muttered to himself. "Parked in a bus lane. Driver under age."

Ms Wiz stepped out of the dodgem and Podge noticed that, while they had been travelling, her clothes had changed from a torn T-shirt to a smart grey suit. "I'm sorry about our parking, officer," she said. "We had to stop here because we're looking for an animal hospital."

"Oh yeah?" The policeman drew himself up to his full height. "I don't see no animals."

Without a word, Ms Wiz took the bag containing Henry the goldfish from Jack.

"Look at him, the poor little creature." She held the bag in front of the policeman's face. "He's suffering from Mad Goldfish Disease. Swimming round and round – going bonkers before your very eyes."

"Don't be daft, lady," said the policeman, his eyes following Henry. "All goldfish do that."

"But they don't do this," said Ms Wiz

under her breath, as a distant humming noise could be heard. "You are now feeling very . . . drowsy," she said. "You want . . . to . . . go . . . to . . . sleep."

"I don't believe it," whispered Jack. "She's using Henry to hypnotise the policeman."

Slowly Ms Wiz lowered the bag. The policeman continued to stare into space, his mouth hanging open.

"You are now under my spell," said Ms

Wiz quietly. "You will do everything you are told. Do you understand?"

"Yes, ma'am," said the policeman.

"Please take me to the Prime Minister's house."

"Yes, ma'am."

"Then come back and make sure no one touches our dodgem."

"No, ma'am. I mean, yes, ma'am."

The policeman turned and slowly, like a sleepwalker, made his way past a barrier and into a quiet side road.

"It's Downing Street," whispered Podge, who had seen a street sign. "This is where the Prime Minister lives."

The policeman reached Number Ten, Downing Street and knocked on the door. "Who shall I say is calling, Ma'am?" he asked.

"Ms Wisdom, Mr Peter Harris and Mr Jack Beddows," said Ms Wiz.

A young woman with neat blonde hair and a neat blue suit opened the door.

"Ms Beddows, Mr Jack Peters and Mr Wisdom Harris to see the Prime Minister," said the policeman in a distant voice.

"Great memory," Jack muttered.

"I'm afraid the Prime Minister is too busy to see anyone but—"

"Too busy?" Ms Wiz pushed forward. "This is important. What's he doing?"

"He's just . . . busy," said the woman, her smile becoming less friendly. "The country doesn't just run itself, you know. Now, my name's Marjorie and I'm from the Prime Minister's office – I'm sure I can help you."

"I don't think so," said Ms Wiz. "This is a highly confidential matter."

"Then in that case, I suggest you write a letter and . . . and . . ." As a faint hum could be heard, Marjorie stopped speaking and stood as motionlessly as if she had been frozen.

"Sorry, Marje," said Ms Wiz, stepping past her into the house. "I'll just have to put a statue spell on you for the moment."

Jack looked nervously at Podge. "I've never seen her this determined," he muttered, as they followed her into the house.

"Now," said Ms Wiz, looking around the dark hall of Number Ten, Downing Street, "I wonder where the person in charge is."

"Why, that must be me."

A man in a dark suit stood at the foot of the stairs in front of them. "Would you mind telling me what you're doing in my house?" he said.

Podge gulped. "It's the P-P-Prime—"

"He looks smaller than he does on telly," said Jack.

Ms Wiz smiled politely. "Marjorie told us you were too busy to see us."

"She was right," said the Prime Minister.

"And we have a problem," said Ms Wiz, extending her hand backwards towards Jack. "He's called Henry."

"Henry?"

"Yes." Ms Wiz held the plastic bag before

the Prime Minister's eyes. "Just look at him." Henry swam round and round and round . . . "You want to go . . . to . . . sleep."

"Why—" The Prime Minister swayed slightly as he spoke in a distant voice. "Why it's a . . . goldfish."

"Prime Minister," said Ms Wiz. "You are now in my power."

CHAPTER THREE
Order! Order!

At 15 Rylett Road, Podge's father Cuthbert
Harris was crouched over a pile of wood
with a screwdriver in his hand.

"This new desk I've bought will be a
surprise for the lad," he was saying to Mrs
Harris, who watched him as he tried to
make sense of the instructions. "It shows
that we're doing our bit. He works harder,
loses his story books, goes on a diet, gives
up chocolate biscuits, says goodbye to his
friends and leaves his school, we buy him
a desk. That's fair, isn't it?" He frowned.
"Now I wonder how this leg goes."

Without a word, Mrs Harris took the
screwdriver from her husband and began
to assemble the desk.

"Action, that's the thing," said Mr
Harris, leaning against the wall. "In this

life, there are doers and watchers. I want our lad to do things – like his father."

"Pass me that screw, will you, Cuthbert," said Mrs Harris, who was already on the second leg of the desk.

"The lad's got to learn. It's dog-eat-dog out there."

"Talking of learning—" Mrs Harris reached for the third leg "—why have you taken Peter's books from his shelves?"

"I'm chucking them out," said Mr

Harris. "They're just stories. Those bookshelves will be needed for the exam guides I've bought." He reached inside a plastic bag beside him. "There's *Mathematics for Exams*, *Geography for Exams*, *English for Exams*." He opened one of the books.

Mrs Harris picked up the fourth leg of the desk.

"Listen to this, Mother." Mr Harris stabbed a fat finger at the book in his hand.

"It says here, 'Welcome to *English for Exams*. This little guide will help you pass your English tests. The most important thing to remember is that the more books you read, the better you'll be at English.' " Mr Harris frowned, then continued, " 'It doesn't matter what books you read so long as you enjoy . . .' " His voice trailed off.

"Interesting." Mrs Harris smiled to herself as she screwed in the desk's last leg.

"Oh, all right." Podge's father shrugged impatiently. "I suppose Peter can keep his books if he likes."

Mrs Harris stood up and looked at her work with satisfaction. "I wonder where he's got to?" she said.

At that moment, Podge was sitting between Ms Wiz and Jack at a long, shiny table in the Cabinet Room at Number Ten, Downing Street. Facing them was the Prime Minister

"So that's our problem, Prime

Minister," Ms Wiz was saying. "All we
need you to do is pass a law that will
prevent Mr Harris taking Podge away from
St Barnabas."

The Prime Minister smiled. "I'm glad you
raised that point," he said. "But, at the
end of the day, we're not playing on a level
playing-field. Someone has moved the goal-
posts. We're in a whole different ball game."

"I beg your pardon?" Ms Wiz looked confused.

"Don't panic, Ms Wiz," said Jack quietly. "This is just the way politicians talk. You have to ask the question again."

"Can you please help us, Prime Minister?"

"That's a very good question," said the Prime Minister. "But, as I've said on a number of occasions, there's a whole range of options and—"

Ms Wiz banged the table. "Yes or no, PM?"

"Er . . . no."

"Why not?" Podge asked. "You're meant to be the person in charge."

"Parliament," said the Prime Minister. "Laws have to go through Parliament."

For a moment there was silence in the Cabinet Room. "That's it then," said Podge eventually. "Not even Ms Wiz could hynotise the whole of Parliament."

"Unless . . ." An odd smile had appeared on the Prime Minister's face. "Unless someone came with me to the Houses of

Parliament this afternoon. Someone who could make a speech."

"Ms Wiz," said Podge.

"No no," said Ms Wiz. "I couldn't possibly. I don't think magic and politics mix."

"Come on," said Jack. "You've taught Class Three. It would be a piece of cake after that."

"Do it for me," begged Podge.

"I think you'd do it very well," said the Prime Minister. "I'll introduce you to the House of Commons and Marjorie can look after Podge and Jack, if you'll just let her move around again."

Ms Wiz sighed. "Oh, all right," she said. "Just a *little* speech."

"Yeah!" said Jack. "Vote for Ms Wiz!"

"Order, order!"

Thirty minutes later, Podge and Jack were looking down on the House of

Commons from a high balcony where they had been taken by Marjorie.

"The government MPs are on one side and the opposition MPs are on the other," Marjorie whispered. "The person in the wig, who keeps saying 'Order, order', is called the Speaker. She's meant to keep everyone under control."

"She's not doing much of a job," muttered Jack. "I've seen more order in the last Assembly of term at St Barnabas."

"But where's the Prime Minister? Where's Ms Wiz?" asked Podge.

As he spoke, an odd growling sound came from the MPs below them. They seemed to be looking towards the door.

"Here they come," said Marjorie.

Slowly the Prime Minister made his way between the rows of MPs. Pale but dignified, Ms Wiz followed him. As they took their seats on the front bench, the Speaker pointed towards them.

"Pray silence for the Prime Minister," she said loudly.

The Prime Minister stood up. "Er, actually," he said, "I'm not going to make a speech this afternoon—"

"Good!" shouted one of the MPs opposite.

"Run out of words, have you?" laughed another.

"How rude," said Podge. "I hope they're not this mean to Ms Wiz."

"Instead, I've asked my good friend Ms Wiz to speak on my behalf."

An astonished silence descended on the chamber.

Ms Wiz rose to her feet. "Thanks, PM," she said. "Now, the reason why I've decided to talk to you this afternoon is that I want you to pass a law to help a boy called Peter Harris."

"Order, order," the Speaker interrupted. "What on earth is going on here? You can't just wander in here and announce that you want to make a law—"

A faint humming sound filled the House of Commons.

"Hoo hoo hoo."

The children stared at the Speaker in amazement. In her place, there now sat a small grey monkey jumping up and down angrily.

One of the MPs on the front bench facing Ms Wiz stood up. "I must object to a complete stranger coming into the House and somehow replacing Madam Speaker with a monkey. This is absolutely . . . whaaaahhhahhhaahhh."

In his place stood a gorilla, thumping his chest.

"Uh-oh," said Jack. "Something tells me Ms Wiz is losing control of this situation."

"Now Peter Harris likes his—" Ms Wiz raised her voice above the noise of interruptions "—he likes his food—". Every MP who stood up to say something was turned into a different kind of monkey.

Soon her words were being drowned by

the noise of chattering, angry, scratching monkeys.

Ms Wiz looked about her and frowned. "We shall return," she said, pulling the Prime Minister to his feet and backing towards the door. "We shall work on our speech at Number Ten, Downing Street."

"I suppose that's it then," said Jack, getting to his feet. "We'd better go home."

Podge followed gloomily. "Ms Wiz was right about one thing," he said. "Politics and magic don't mix."

CHAPTER FOUR

A Message from the PM

The Prime Minister's car moved slowly through the crowds that had gathered outside the Houses of Parliament.

On the back seat Podge and Jack sat between the Prime Minister and Marjorie. Ms Wiz was in the front, waving to the crowd.

"What's happened to Ms Wiz?" Jack whispered to Podge. "One speech to the House of Commons and suddenly she's behaving like she's the Queen or something."

"And it wasn't exactly the greatest speech ever made," grumbled Podge. "We'll never get my dad to change his mind now."

"Cameras, television, that's what you want," said the Prime Minister in a strange, dreamlike voice.

"Oh, Prime Minister—" Ms Wiz smiled modestly. "All this fame – and so soon."

"I meant for Podge," said the Prime Minister. "If we want his parents to change their mind, we'll need publicity. Television."

"That's it!" Jack turned to Podge. "If you appeared on television, your dad would *have* to pay attention. You'd be the week's good cause – Podge-Aid."

"Marjorie, I want to speak to the nation with Ms Wiz," said the Prime Minister suddenly. "In half an hour's time."

"B-but, sir." Marjorie had turned pale. "We're only meant to do that when there's a national emergency."

"This is an emergency. Podge is being forced to leave St Barnabas."

"Anyway," said Marjorie, "it's a terrible time to appear on television – everyone will be waiting to watch that daily soap opera, *The Avenue*."

"Dad's favourite programme!" said Podge.

"Perfect." The Prime Minister smiled. "Get the cameras round as soon as we arrive."

"My speech!" In the front seat, Ms Wiz stopped waving for a moment. "I must work on my speech."

"Crazy," sighed Jack.

Mr Harris was exhausted. He had helped Mrs Harris while she was assembling the desk. He had watched while she tidied all the books in the bedroom. He had stood by, offering advice while Mrs Harris worked out a diet that would help produce a lean, mean Peter Harris.

"Phew," he said, flopping into an armchair in front of the television. "Any chance of a cup of tea, Mother?"

"No, Cuthbert." Mrs Harris sat down beside him. "I made the desk. You make

the tea. There's just time before *The Avenue*."

Grumbling, Mr Harris stood up. "Work, work, work," he muttered.

"I can't think where Peter's got to," said Mrs Harris. "He was meant to be back an hour ago."

"Having too much fun probably," Mr Harris called out from the kitchen. "There'll be an end to that with the new school."

Grumbling, he returned to the sitting room and switched on the television.

"There's now a change to the advertised programme," said the TV announcer. "Instead of *The Avenue*, we'll be going over live in a few moments to Number Ten, Downing Street for a message from the Prime Minister."

"Oh *no!*" said Mr Harris.

The Prime Minister's office was lit up by television lights.

A rather large television producer, called Miss Barkworth, was fussing around with the papers on the Prime Minister's desk. "This is all most irregular, sir," she said. "We haven't even been given a script for you to read from the autocue."

"What's an autocue?" Jack asked Podge as they watched the preparations.

"It's the little screen they read from

when they're making a speech on telly," Podge whispered.

"I don't need a script," the Prime Minister was telling the producer. "My colleague Ms Wiz will be doing most of the talking."

"But who is this Wiz person?" The producer lowered her voice as she saw Ms Wiz pacing nervously backwards and forwards in the office. "Has she ever done any public speaking?"

"She spoke to the House of Commons this afternoon," said the Prime Minister. "An excellent speech, it was."

"Yeah," muttered Jack. "She made monkeys of them."

Ms Wiz stood in front of the mirror, rehearsing her lines. "Ladies and gentlemen," she said, then frowned. "No, too serious . . . Hullo, everybody! No, that's wrong . . . Hi, my name's Ms Wiz—"

"Just be yourself," smiled Podge. "You'll be fine."

"Thirty seconds before we're on air," shouted Miss Barkworth, scurrying behind the camera. "I want the PM at his desk, Ms Wiz standing beside him and the fat boy a bit to the left."

"She's not exactly Miss Skinny herself," murmured Jack as he moved out of camera range.

"Sshh!" The producer held up five fingers, then four ... three ... two ... one ...

The Prime Minister switched on his most sincere smile as a red light appeared above the camera.

"Hullo," he said. "I expect you're all wondering why I decided to speak to the nation this afternoon ..."

A Lady not for Turning

Mr Harris sat grumpily in front of the television set, a mug of tea in his hand.

"Politicians!" he said to Mrs Harris. "You work hard, you do your best for your lad. All you ask in return is the chance to relax in front of *The Avenue*. But no—"

"It must be something really important," said Mrs Harris. "People don't interrupt *The Avenue* for nothing."

"Publicity, Mother." Mr Harris slurped his tea. "Your average politician will do anything for publicity."

"And so," the Prime Minister was saying on television, "I would now like to hand you over to my friend and colleague, Ms Wiz."

"Ms Wiz?" Mr Harris sat forward in his chair. "Isn't that the woman who turned

up at St Barnabas and sent a rat up the
school inspector's trousers?"

"What on earth is she doing there?"
asked Mrs Harris.

"I always knew that woman spelt
trouble—"

"Shush, Cuthbert," said Mrs Harris.
"Let's hear what she has to say."

Ms Wiz sat easily on the edge of the
Prime Minister's desk. "This afternoon I
want to tell you the story of a little boy," she
said. "Just an ordinary lad. He likes his
books. He likes his friends. He likes his
chocolate biscuits."

As she smiled, the camera moved closer
to her face.

"Yet this little boy's father has decided to
drag him away from his school, his lovely
childhood friends—"

"Poor little mite," said Mr Harris.

"—his nice stories—"

"What a shame," said Mr Harris.

"—even his chocolate biscuits."

Mr Harris shook his head. "Some parents don't deserve to have children," he said.

"Is this fair?" The woman on the television glanced to her right. "Look at this boy. Is he really so fat?"

She paused as the camera turned to show a child in the shadows of the office.

"Yes, all right, perhaps he is a bit . . . plump," Ms Wiz smiled. "But maybe he eats food as a way of expressing himself, as a way of asking for love from his mum and dad. Maybe every chocolate biscuit that

he eats is not so much a chocolate biscuit as a cry for help—"

"And the little thing looks just like our Peter," sobbed Mrs Harris.

"I don't care who he is." Mr Harris blew his nose on a big red handkerchief. "That boy's parents should be more understanding."

"So I ask you all today," the woman continued, "listen to your children. They have the right to have friends, books – even chocolate biscuits now and then. Let the

example of Podge Harris be an example to us all."

Mr and Mrs Harris stopped crying and stared at one another in amazement.

"Podge Harris?" they said.

The cameras had left Number Ten, Downing Street but Ms Wiz was behaving more and more strangely.

"Where are my ministers?" she asked, looking about her as she sat at the Prime Minister's desk. "I want to go to Parliament and make some laws."

"You did brilliantly, Ms Wiz," said Podge. "But I think we ought to be on our way home. Our parents will be getting worried."

"Home?" Ms Wiz looked shocked. "But my work here has just begun. This lady is not for turning."

"I'm starving," muttered Podge.

"Now, PM—" Ms Wiz beckoned to the

back of the room where the Prime Minister stood with Marjorie and Miss Barkworth. "I'd like to discuss some new laws that we'll be making."

"But Ms Wiz—" The Prime Minister smiled politely. "You've turned most of Parliament into monkeys."

"The spell will have worn off by now," said Ms Wiz. "But I could do it again if you like. Yes, that's a good idea. If people disagree with us, I'll just change them into monkeys."

"What are we going to do with her?" Podge whispered to Jack. "She's gone power-crazy."

Jack was staring at Henry the goldfish, whose plastic bag he had put on a bookshelf nearby. "What we need is a bit of magic to help us. A bit of Henry magic." He picked up the bag. "Oh no, Ms Wiz," he said loudly. "Look what's happened."

Frowning, Ms Wiz turned. "What's the problem, Jack?" she asked.

"It's Henry. He's been dazzled by the television lights." He held the fish up in front of Ms Wiz's eyes. "Ms Wiz," he said, "You want to go . . . to . . . sleep."

Ms Wiz stared straight ahead of her.

Podge gulped. "I don't believe it!" he gasped. "You've hypnotised Ms Wiz."

"She said Henry had his own magic. I thought it might work on her and it did." Jack smiled. "Ms Wiz, you are now going to say goodbye to the Prime Minister," he said.

"Goodbye, Prime Minister," said Ms Wiz in a sleepy voice.

"Goodbye, Ms Wiz," said the Prime Minister.

"You will ask him to pass a law banning all schools."

"Jack!" Podge grabbed his arm. "Don't mess about – let's go home."

"That was a joke, Ms Wiz," said Jack quickly. "Please take us back to the purple dodgem and then fly us home."

"Anything you say, Jack," said Ms Wiz.

They walked slowly towards the front door. "Shouldn't you take the spell off the Prime Minister?" Marjorie asked. "Otherwise he'll be staring into space and talking like a computer for ever."

Jack looked at the Prime Minister for a moment. "I don't think anyone will notice the difference," he said.

"Thanks, PM," Podge shouted back.

"Good luck, Podge," said the Prime Minister, closing the door of Number Ten, Downing Street behind them.

The purple dodgem hovered just above 15 Rylett Road before landing gently on the Harrises' carefully tended lawn.

"Peter!" Mrs Harris opened the front door. "We were so worried about you."

Mr Harris appeared behind his wife. "We saw you on telly, son. You looked great."

"Dad's been thinking," said Mrs Harris, nudging her husband.

"Have I?" Mr Harris frowned. "Oh yes."
He placed his arm around Podge's
shoulder. "Son," he said, "maybe I was a
bit . . . hasty this morning."

"You mean about the books and the
biscuits and St Barnabas?" asked Podge.

"That's right." Mr Harris managed a
smile.

"Yeah," said Jack. "Good old Mr Harris!
And it's all thanks to Ms Wiz."

They turned to the purple dodgem

where Ms Wiz was still sitting motionlessly.

"What's the matter with her, Jack?" asked Mrs Harris.

"I think she's just feeling a bit tired," said Jack, walking over to the dodgem. He clicked his fingers in front of Ms Wiz's eyes.

"Wha – what?" Ms Wiz shook her head and rubbed her eyes, as if she were just waking up. "I had this weird dream that I went crazy for power."

"Unbelievable," said Jack.

"And—" Ms Wiz started laughing, "I even thought Podge was being taken away from St Barnabas and put on a diet."

"Ridiculous," said Mr Harris.

"Oh well, so long as it was just a dream," said Ms Wiz. "I'd better get this back to the fair." There was a faint humming noise as she drove the purple dodgem back to the road. "I think I'll go by road to the fairground," she said. "The traffic isn't too bad."

"Drive carefully, Ms Wiz," said Podge. "And thank you."

"Bye, Podge. Bye, Jack," she called out. "Bye, Mr and Mrs Harris."

With a roar of the engine, she accelerated away and within seconds had turned the corner of the street and disappeared. For a moment, Mr and Mrs Harris and the children listened as the scream of tyres faded in the distance.

"She may be magic but she's no driver," muttered Mr Harris.

Podge turned into the house. "I'm starving," he said.

"Oh, Peter," said Mrs Harris.

"What about that diet then, son?" Mr Harris asked.

"Podge." Jack stepped forward, holding Henry the goldfish in front of him. "Watch the fishy, please."

Podge hesitated, then followed Henry with his eyes as he swam round and round.

"Can you hear me?" said Jack.

"Yeees." Podge's voice was strange and lifeless. "I can hear you, O master."

"Say after me – I want to go . . . to . . . sleep."

"I want . . . I want . . . I want . . . I want a chocolate biscuit."

Jack shrugged at Mr and Mrs Harris as Podge made for the kitchen.

"Sometimes the magic takes a little time to work," he said.

Ms Wiz
Loves Dracula

*This book is dedicated to
all the children who have written
to me about Ms Wiz.*

Acknowledgements

*I would like to thank Salvatore Genco,
Andrea Kaizer and Darren Wade of East-
field Primary School, Enfield, whose own
Ms Wiz story was the original inspiration
for this book, and all the pupils of
Mowbray County Junior School, South
Shields, for their helpful comments on the
story itself.*

CHAPTER ONE

A Load of Parents
Getting Drunk

It was the end of the last day of autumn
term at St Barnabas School. Children were
running across the playground to be met by
their parents at the school gate. From the
gym nearby could be heard the sound of a
radio playing. Tonight was the night of the
Christmas fancy-dress dance held by the
PTA, and some of the teachers were
putting up the decorations.

With their satchels slung over their
shoulders, Jack Beddows and Lizzie
Thompson stood at the doorway of the gym
and watched as Class Three's teacher, Mr
Bailey, climbed a stepladder to attach
balloons to the wall bars.

"Call themselves the Parent Teacher
Association," said Jack. "All they want to do
is prance about in fancy dress."

Lizzie smiled. "Miss Gomaz told Class Four that she was going as Teddy Edward. There's a rumour that Mr Gilbert's hired a Superman costume."

"Is it a bird? Is it a plane?" said Jack in his favourite American accent. "No, it's the head teacher of St Barnabas School in a silly suit."

"I wonder what Mr Bailey's going as," whispered Lizzie.

"A ghost, probably," said Jack. "He'd

look all right with a sheet over his head."

As if he had heard their conversation, Mr Bailey glanced over and saw the two children standing in the doorway. "Off you go, you two," he called out. "It's the grown-ups' time now."

"Bye, sir," Jack called out. "Don't forget to dance with Teddy Edward."

It was getting dark as Jack and Lizzie made their way across the school play-

ground and out of the gate towards Lizzie's house where Jack was staying that night.

"I know it's only a stupid fancy-dress dance but I really wish we were going," Jack said. "I'd give anything to see Mr Gilbert as the Man of Steel."

"And we've got Helen from next door babysitting," said Lizzie gloomily. "She's really strict about when we go to bed."

"If only we had—" Jack had been just about to say, "If only we had Ms Wiz as a babysitter," when he saw a familiar figure sitting on a wall across the road from the school. She was wearing a long overcoat and a woolly hat, but that dark hair was unmistakable. "Look who it is," he said.

"I don't believe it," said Lizzie. "She hasn't visited us for ages."

"Ms Wiz!" Jack shouted as they ran towards a zebra crossing nearby, but the figure continued to look down at the pavement, deep in thought.

"She doesn't look very happy,"

murmured Lizzie as they approached.
"Perhaps she's lost her magic."

"Yo, Ms Wiz," Jack called out.

Ms Wiz looked up, as if awakening from
a daydream. "Hi, Jack," she smiled. "Hi,
Lizzie."

"We were just talking about you," said
Jack. "I'm staying with Lizzie tonight and
we need a babysitter."

"Yeah, it's unfair," said Lizzie. "My
mum and Jack's parents are going to the

PTA fancy-dress dance and we have to stay at home with the world's strictest babysitter."

"Fancy dress?" Suddenly Ms Wiz looked interested. "That sounds fun."

"Nah, you'd hate it," said Jack. "It's just a load of parents getting drunk and dancing with teachers to really old sixties songs."

"Great." Ms Wiz jumped down off the wall. "Where can I get a ticket?"

Mrs Thompson was in a bad mood. Lizzie and Jack had promised not to be late back from school, and they were. The shop where she had hired a nurse's uniform for tonight's dance had promised it would fit her, and it didn't. She was looking at herself in the hall mirror when the bell rang.

"Glad you could make it," she said, opening the door to Lizzie and Jack.

Lizzie looked at her mother in the nurse's uniform. "Er, you look great, Mum," she said eventually.

"Yeah, dig Florence Nightingale," said Jack in a serious attempt at politeness.

"I look ridiculous," moaned Mrs Thompson. "I'm all . . . bulgy."

From the darkness behind Jack and Lizzie could be heard a faint humming sound.

"What's happening?" Mrs Thompson looked down at her uniform which seemed to be slowly expanding. After a few seconds, the material stopped moving. It was now a perfect fit.

"Is that any better?" asked Ms Wiz, stepping out of the shadows.

"This is Ms Wiz," said Lizzie. "You remember the Paranormal Operative who used to visit Class Three? Well, she's back and, as you can see, her magic's still working."

"Paranormal Operative? Magic?" Mrs

Thompson looked from the nurse's uniform to Ms Wiz. "The costume won't shrink back at the wrong moment, will it?" she asked nervously. "I don't want to go all bulgy again just when I'm dancing with Mr Gilbert."

Ms Wiz laughed. "No," she said. "Anyway, I'll be there to make sure the spell keeps working."

"Will you?" Mrs Thompson looked surprised.

"Ms Wiz wants to go to the dance," Lizzie explained.

"Weren't you banned once from St Barnabas?" asked Mrs Thompson. "Something about sending a class on a field trip to the other side of the world?"

Ms Wiz shrugged. "It was a long time ago. Anyway, no one will recognize me in fancy dress."

"I'm not sure." Mrs Thompson frowned as she turned towards the kitchen. "Will you promise not to do any of your spells?" she asked.

"Trust me," said Ms Wiz.

"Oh, all right," said Mrs Thompson. "You can change in my room upstairs."

"But what will you change into?" Lizzie asked.

Ms Wiz smiled. "I'll think of something," she said.

"There's one thing I don't understand," said Jack, after Ms Wiz had gone to change. "Whenever Ms Wiz comes to see us, she tells us that she goes where magic is needed."

"That's true," said Lizzie. "There's always a problem that needs solving when she turns up."

"So who is it who needs the magic now?" asked Jack. There was silence in the kitchen as the three of them thought about this.

"Perhaps it's Ms Wiz herself who needs the magic," said Mrs Thompson eventually.

"Ms Wiz need magic?" Jack laughed. "Never."

"She might be lonely," said Mrs Thompson. "That would explain why she's so keen on going to the dance."

"Maybe she's looking for a boyfriend," said Lizzie.

Jack laughed. "Don't be ridiculous," he said. "Ms Wiz isn't like that – anyway she's got Herbert the rat for company."

"A rat's not quite the same as a boyfriend," said Lizzie.

"Hmm," said Mrs Thompson. "No comment."

There was a rustling sound from the stairs. A dark, wild-haired witch dressed in stylish black off-the-shoulder rags, her green eyes sparkling, made her way slowly down the stairs.

"How do I look?" asked Ms Wiz.

CHAPTER TWO
Strangers in the Night

Before Dracula arrived, it had been a PTA
dance like any other PTA dance. There was
soggy quiche. There was wine which even
Mrs Hicks, who could drink almost
anything, had difficulty in swallowing. One
of the dads had already hurt his back
doing the twist. In spite of all Mr Bailey's
efforts, the gym didn't really look like a
disco – it looked like a gym with a few
balloons hanging from the walls.

Ms Wiz stood with Lizzie's mother near
the Christmas tree. She wanted to dance
but the fathers seemed to be too nervous to
speak to her.

"I think they recognize me," she
whispered to Mrs Thompson. "They're
worried I'll bewitch them or something."

Mrs Thompson glanced at Ms Wiz. "The

trouble is we're not used to such glamorous witches at St Barnabas," she said. "We have this idea that a witch should be an old girl with a hunchback, long dirty fingernails, and a drip on the end of her crooked nose."

"How very old-fashioned," sighed Ms Wiz, smiling at a small figure in a strange costume who was now approaching them.

"Hullo, I'm the head teacher," said Mr Gilbert, shaking Ms Wiz's hand. He gave a nervous little laugh. "Except tonight I'm Superman."

"Ah yes," said Mz Wiz, who had been wondering why he was wearing blue pyjamas and a little red cape. "Pleased to meet you, Superman."

"Now, I can't help feeling we've met somewhere before," said Mr Gilbert.

"I don't think so," said Ms Wiz quickly. "My name's—"

It was at that precise moment that the music stopped and the lights went out.

There were groans from around the gym. "Not *another* power cut," said a voice in the darkness. "That's the third time the electricity's gone off this week."

Someone standing by the doorway lit a match. The door behind him opened to reveal a tall, dark figure with glittering eyes. Two long incisor teeth protruded slightly over his lower lip.

"Got a torch, Count Dracula?" laughed one of the parents.

The figure in black said nothing.

"Typical," laughed Lizzie's mother, as Mr Gilbert hurried away to find some candles. "Something like this always happens at the PTA dance. But at least it saved you from having to dance with Superman."

"Mmm?" Ms Wiz was staring across the room.

"That man's got the heaviest feet—" Mrs Thompson realized that Ms Wiz was no

longer listening to her. "Have you seen someone you know?"

A hint of colour had come to Ms Wiz's cheeks. "I think I've just seen the vampire of my dreams," she said.

Lizzie wasn't tired. Nor was Jack. They sat in Lizzie's room listening to the television downstairs and wondering what was happening at the PTA dance.

"My mum says that when you can't sleep, you should get up and walk around a bit," said Lizzie.

Jack thought about this for a moment. "Perhaps we could walk down the road to St Barnabas. The fresh air would do us good. We could take a look at the dance through the window of the gym."

"What about Helen, downstairs?" Lizzie whispered.

"We'll only be gone a few minutes. She's probably asleep in front of the telly."

Without another word, the two children dressed.

"This is bad," muttered Lizzie as, a few minutes later, they stood at the top of the stairs. "My mum'll kill me if she sees us."

They crept downstairs, silently lifted the spare front door key off a hook in the hall and let themselves out of the house into the dark night.

It had been one of the strangest dances she had ever been to, Lizzie's mother thought as she danced with Mr Harris. First of all, when the electricity had come back on, there had been an odd humming noise from the direction of Ms Wiz. Suddenly the lights in the gym had dimmed, giving it a soft, romantic glow.

"That's better," Ms Wiz had said. Without another word, she had walked across the room and had introduced herself to Dracula.

Then there was the music. Normally it was loud and fast at the PTA dance but, when Ms Wiz had first walked onto the dance floor with Dracula, she had glanced at the cassette player, there had been another humming noise – and, from then on, the only music the machine would play was slow, smoochy Frank Sinatra songs, to which Ms Wiz and Dracula danced all evening.

Not that the music made any difference to Mr Harris, Mrs Thompson sighed to herself. As usual, he was pushing her around the dance floor like a removal man delivering a cupboard on his last shift. Over his shoulder, Mrs Thompson smiled as she saw Dracula and Ms Wiz dancing slowly in one of the darker corners.

"It's all very strange indeed," she murmured.

"What's that, love?" Mr Harris barked in her ear.

"Um, it's strange how well you dance," said Mrs Thompson quickly.

"Oh yes, I like a good old stomp," said Mr Harris, treading hard on her right toe.

As the song ended, Ms Wiz and Dracula slipped out of the gym and into the playground.

"I'd better be going home now," said Dracula in a deep, silky voice.

"Of course," Ms Wiz smiled cheerfully. "The last train for Transylvania must be leaving soon."

"Perhaps we could, you know . . ." Dracula seemed to be lost for words. "D'you fancy going to the cinema some time?"

Ms Wiz laughed. "Afternoon show, I suppose. You must be busy at night."

"Busy?"

"Night shift. All that flying about with the other vampires."

"Yes, of course." Dracula sighed. "It does keep me busy."

For a moment, there was an awkward silence in the playground, except for the sound of "Strangers in the Night" drifting across from the gym.

"Well," said Ms Wiz softly. "It's been a great pleasure." She shook Dracula's hand and turned away.

"What did you say your name was?" Dracula called out.

"Ms Wiz. But you can call me Dolores."

"Can I telephone you?"

Ms Wiz hesitated. "I'm not on the telephone, I'm afraid," she said. "But I

suppose you could leave a message for me with Lizzie's mother, Mrs Thompson." She waved and walked into the gym.

"Who's Lizzie? Who's Mrs Thompson?" murmured Dracula to himself. "Oh, I'll never see that beautiful witch again." He took a handkerchief out of his top pocket and blew his nose. Then, slowly and sadly, he walked out of the school gates and down the road.

*

"Talk about embarrassing," said Jack, emerging from the shadows nearby. "For one moment, I thought they were going to kiss or something gross like that."

"They couldn't," said Lizzie. "His teeth would get in the way, wouldn't they?" Glancing down, she noticed a small white card on the ground. "He dropped something," she said, picking it up. "It says 'College of National Assessment'. Then there's an address. Maybe he wasn't Dracula after all."

"Of course he was," said Jack. "I mean, he wouldn't go around with cards saying 'DRACULA – VAMPIRE AND BLOODSUCKING NEEDS – ESTIMATES FREE', would he? That card's just to throw people off his track."

Lizzie was walking towards the school gate. "He seemed a bit shy for a vampire," she said.

"That was a vampire, all right," said Jack. "Can you imagine Ms Wiz dancing the night away with just an ordinary bloke in a silly fancy dress?"

"I don't know," said Lizzie. "I don't seem to know anything about Ms Wiz any more."

CHAPTER THREE

A Gorgeous, Hunky Lord of the Undead

A low moaning sound could be heard coming from the kitchen when Lizzie and Jack came down to breakfast the following morning.

"Oh no," Lizzie sighed. Mrs Thompson was sitting at the kitchen table, her head in her hands, staring into a cup of coffee.

"Your mum looks really ill," whispered Jack.

"It's what's called a hangover," said Lizzie, speaking as loudly as before. "Every year Mum goes to the PTA dance and every year she has this special PTA dance hangover from drinking too much."

"Someone must have put something in the wine, I only had two glasses," muttered Mrs Thompson, as she looked up

at the children with small, bloodshot eyes.

"It's called alcohol, Mum," said Lizzie.

"Where's Ms Wiz?" asked Jack, anxious
to change the subject.

"Flew home after the dance," said Mrs
Thompson. She sipped at her coffee. "I
think she lost her heart to Dracula."

"Her heart? Ugh, you mean he just took
it?" said Jack. "Didn't it make a mess on
the dance floor?"

Mrs Thompson laughed, then winced.

"No jokes," she begged. "Don't make me laugh."

"It wasn't really Dracula, was it?" asked Lizzie, thinking of the card she had picked up in the playground.

"No one knew who he was." Mrs Thompson stood up slowly. "Wasn't a parent, wasn't a teacher. Maybe Ms Wiz thought the PTA dance was a Bring Your Own Vampire party."

The front doorbell rang loudly.

"I wonder who that could be," said Lizzie.

Mrs Thompson was tottering towards the stairs. "Tell them to go away. I'm off back to bed," she muttered, as Jack and Lizzie ran to the front door.

An extraordinary sight greeted their eyes. Ms Wiz, wearing a pink T-shirt covered with purple hearts, was hovering six inches above the ground. A cloud of beautiful yellow butterflies flitted around her head.

"Jack! Lizzie!" she exclaimed in a

strange, fluting voice. "I was passing by and I just wanted to tell you that it's an absolutely *wonderful* morning."

Lizzie held the front door open as Ms Wiz floated into the house, followed by the yellow butterflies.

"Are you feeling all right, Ms Wiz?" Jack asked. "Why aren't your feet on the ground? You look all . . . weird."

"Weird? *Moi?*" Ms Wiz smiled dreamily. "I've never felt better in my life. I suppose there aren't any—" she fluttered her eyelashes "—messages for me."

"What sort of messages?" asked Lizzie.

"You know, little notes written in blood which have been popped through the letterbox. Maybe a present – a dead bat perhaps or—"

"From Dracula, you mean," said Jack.

"Dracula?" Ms Wiz smiled innocently.

"Everybody knows about you and Dracula," said Lizzie. "You were the talk of the PTA dance."

Ms Wiz flew around the hall, singing out, "My head's in a spin, my heart's on fire, I've fallen in love with a bloodsucking vampire."

"Er, Ms Wiz—" said Jack.

"We'll stay together, we'll never part, my love for Drax is like a stake through my heart."

"Ms Wiz, I think—" said Lizzie, trying to interrupt.

"Blood is red, veins are blue, his fangs are pearly and—"

"Ms Wiz!" shouted Jack. "Stop floating about the hall spouting poetry, and just think about this. You cannot fall in love with a vampire."

Ms Wiz paused mid-flight. "Why not?" she smiled. "This is the real thing at last."

"Yes, but is *he* a real thing?" asked Lizzie. "After all, you did meet him at a fancy dress dance. Maybe he's not a real vampire."

"Of course he is," Ms Wiz smiled. "I'd

know a vampire anywhere. Those cute, long nails. Those dark, sweet, evil eyes."

"All right, let's say he is Dracula," said Jack. "He's not exactly going to be a perfect boyfriend, is he? I mean, think of all that bloodsucking. After a few nights out with him, your neck would be like a pin-cushion."

Ms Wiz frowned and touched her neck nervously. Then she shrugged. "Oh, fiddle-di-dee," she said. "What's a bit of bloodsucking between friends?"

"Then there's the garlic," said Lizzie. "When you go out to a restaurant, you'll always have to worry about what's in the meal. Vampires hate garlic."

"The course of love never did run smooth," smiled Ms Wiz. "Even with a gorgeous, hunky Lord of the Undead."

"And think of Class Three," said Jack desperately. "Can you imagine how upset they'll be when they hear you're dating a vampire?"

"That's no problem," said Ms Wiz. "You can all come and visit us in Count Dracula's dark, crumbling castle in Transylvania."

Lizzie reached into the back pocket of her jeans. She didn't want to upset Ms Wiz but it was time for a bit of reality. "He doesn't actually live in Transylvania," she said. "He dropped his card in the playground. The Lord of the Undead seems to live at 43, Addison Gardens."

"The neighbours must be pleased," muttered Jack.

For the first time, Ms Wiz floated down to earth. "You . . . you have the address of my beloved?" she asked faintly. "We must go there right now."

"Promise you won't be disappointed?" asked Lizzie.

"Take me to my fanged one," said Ms Wiz, hovering by the front door.

Lizzie looked at Jack, who shrugged. "Why not?" he said.

"Oh well, it's only five minutes away," sighed Lizzie. Picking up her coat, she called up the stairs, "Mum, we're just going down the road with Ms Wiz on a love quest for a bloodsucking vampire, all right?"

"Mmmm," moaned Mrs Thompson.

43, Addison Gardens was a block of flats. Beside the door were six doorbells with names beside them. None of them was that of Count Dracula.

"It must be the top flat," said Ms Wiz. "Vampires are like bats – they live under the roof."

"We can't just ring the top bell and ask if Dracula's at home," said Lizzie.

"I'll fly up and spy through the window," suggested Ms Wiz.

While they were talking, Jack had crept to a nearby window. Now he beckoned them over urgently.

Through the window could be seen
a small room. A long, black cloak had
been thrown over a chair near the
window. Pacing backwards and forwards
was a tall, good-looking man with dark hair
and glasses. Now and then, he would
pause to look at an object on a table
nearby. They were a set of false vampire's
fangs.

"I recognize him," whispered Lizzie.
"It's the new school inspector."

"You're right," said Jack. "What was his
name? Mr Arnold – that was it. He visited
us at the beginning of term."

"A school inspector?" said Ms Wiz.

"I'm afraid so." Lizzie looked at Ms
Wiz sympathetically. "He wasn't Dracula
after all."

"Look on the bright side," said Jack.
"There'll be other vampires."

A smile had appeared once more on Ms
Wiz's face. She floated off the ground,
singing out, "Ms Wiz was blind, you were

right to correct her, her heart belongs to a school inspector."

"I don't believe it," said Jack.

CHAPTER FOUR
It's Magic or Me

Ever since Lizzie's father had left home
when she was five, Lizzie had been really
close to her mother. She liked seeing her
father at weekends but, when it came to
the real problems in her life, there was only
one person she could talk to.

"We've got a crisis, Mum," she said
as they sat watching television together
a few days later. "People have been
seeing Ms Wiz and Mr Arnold everywhere.
At the cinema. Feeding the ducks in
the park. Podge swears he saw them
walking down the High Street holding
hands."

"Nice." Mrs Thompson was half-
listening, her eyes on the screen. "I'm so
glad he wasn't a real vampire."

"But it's not right for Ms Wiz to be

hanging around the cinema and the park
It's so . . . normal."

"I told you she was lonely," said
Mrs Thompson. "Just because she does a
bit of magic now and then, it doesn't
mean she's not interested in having a
boyfriend."

"But you're not interested in having a
boyfriend," said Lizzie.

"That's because I was married to your
father," said Mrs Thompson, pursing her

lips as if she could say more but didn't want to. "He cured me of men."

"There's an idea," said Lizzie. "Perhaps I could introduce Dad to Ms Wiz on our next weekend together. Maybe he'd cure her too."

Mrs Thompson laughed. "He couldn't handle a normal person, let alone a paranormal operative with rats, china cats and weird spells." She frowned. "I wonder if Mr Arnold knows about all that."

Lizzie thought about this for a moment. Then she leapt to her feet. "Mum, you're a genius," she said, making for the door.

"Where are you going?" asked Mrs Thompson.

"I'm phoning Jack," Lizzie called over her shoulder. "I've just thought of a solution to our crisis."

Brian Arnold walked down the High Street, which was packed with Christmas shoppers. Smiling, he whistled softly to himself. He didn't think he had ever been so happy in his life.

It had been a matter of sheer luck that he had gone to the St Barnabas dance – he had only accepted Mr Gilbert's invitation out of politeness. Yet there, as if by magic, he had met the most beautiful woman in the world.

"Yes, it really was as if by magic," he had said to Ms Wiz on their first date together two days after the dance.

"It wasn't magic, it was life," Ms Wiz had replied with the merest hint of irritation in her voice. "Magic had nothing to do with it." Mr Arnold had never discovered why the word "magic" seemed to upset her so much.

There was another wonderful thing. Mr Arnold loved children – that was why he had become a school inspector – but, until recently, he had rarely been friends with them outside school hours. Ever since he had met Ms Wiz, he always seemed to be meeting children from Class Three. It was almost as if they were following him.

In fact, he was seeing some children this very afternoon. Jack and Lizzie had invited him out for a Christmas hamburger at the Big Burger Bar on the High Street. Ms Wiz had promised to meet them there.

"A lovely girlfriend. Children offering me a Christmas hamburger." Mr Arnold smiled to himself as he opened the door to the Big Burger Bar. "What a lucky man I am."

Jack and Lizzie were already sipping cokes at a corner table.

"This was an excellent idea," he said as he took his seat.

"Mum said we could buy you burgers as a sort of Christmas present," smiled Lizzie.

"Very decent of you," said Mr Arnold. "I wonder where Dolores has got to."

"Dolores?" Jack frowned. "Oh, you mean Ms Wiz. She'll probably fly in on her

vacuum cleaner – just like she did when we first met her at St Barnabas."

"Vacuum cleaner?" The school inspector smiled politely. "How exactly can someone fly on a vacuum cleaner?"

"The same way as someone can turn Podge's father into a warthog. Or Mr Gilbert into a sheep," said Jack. "If that someone happens to have magic powers, like Ms Wiz has."

"Excuse me, children—" Mr Arnold

cleared his throat nervously. "Are you telling me that Dolores – er, Ms Wiz – is . . . not quite as other women?"

"Of course she's not," said Jack. "You mean she never told you? She calls herself a paranormal operative. It's a sort of modern witch." He pulled a small bottle from his pocket. "This little bottle had my appendix in it after I had an operation at the hospital – that is, until Mr Bailey, my teacher, ate it, thanks to a bit of Ms Wiz magic."

"And she's got this rat she keeps under her shirt," said Lizzie. "It ran up the leg of the last school inspector's trousers during a lesson."

Mr Arnold nodded slowly. "So that was why Mr Smith left the job in such a hurry. When I was given his job, I was told that he had problems with his nerves."

"Hi, everyone."

Lizzie, Jack and Mr Arnold turned to see Ms Wiz, waving as she made her way across the restaurant towards them.

"What's the matter?" she said, as she arrived. "You all look as if you've seen a ghost."

"Not a ghost," said Mr Arnold grimly. "But a paranormal operative."

"Ah." Ms Wiz sat down slowly. "You've heard."

"Jack and Lizzie have been telling me all about your spells."

"Thanks, Jack. Thanks, Lizzie." Ms Wiz picked up the menu, as if nothing unusual had happened. "Now, I wonder if they have anything vegetarian here," she said.

"Dolores, I must ask you a question." Mr Arnold sat forward in his seat. "Do you or do you not keep a magic rat in your underwear?"

A faint humming sound came from across the table. "Oh look!" Ms Wiz pointed behind them. "Flying hamburgers!" There were gasps from the diners as hamburgers floated off their plates to swoop around the restaurant, splashing relish, mayonnaise and tomato sauce everywhere. "Isn't that strange, Brian?"

But Mr Arnold ignored the hamburgers. "You're just making it worse by trying to put me off with some sort of conjuring trick," he said. "Tell me about the rat. Do you—?"

A crash of plates, followed by the thud of bodies hitting the ground, interrupted him. "That's odd, Brian," said Ms Wiz desperately. "The floor of the restaurant has been changed into an ice rink. Those poor waiters are falling all over the place."

"The rat, Dolores," said Mr Arnold.

As the humming noise died down, the flying hamburgers settled back onto their plates and the waiters picked themselves up off the floor. Ms Wiz sighed and reached inside her T-shirt, pulling out a small, brown rat which she put on the table. "Tell him, Herbert," she said.

"It's very simple," said the rat, in a squeaky but well-educated voice. "My name is Herbert and I am indeed a magic rat. I would like to take this opportunity to apologize profusely for running up your former colleague's trousers."

There was a scream from a nearby table. "A rat!" With a trembling hand, a woman pointed to Herbert. "And it's talking!"

"Yeah, yeah!" said Herbert, glancing casually in her direction. "Now, as I was saying—"

Mr Arnold had heard enough. He pushed back his chair and stood up. "That's it, Dolores," he said to Ms Wiz. "Call me old-fashioned but I'm not going out with someone who makes hamburgers fly off plates and goes around with talking rats in her undergarments." He backed towards the door. "You have to choose, Dolores – it's magic or me." Without another word, he blundered out of the door and into the street outside.

"Whoops," said Jack.

"I'm sorry, Ms Wiz." Lizzie laid a hand on Ms Wiz's arm. "We shouldn't have told him about your magic."

"Never mind." Ms Wiz smiled bravely. "He had to find out some time." She sighed. "Oh well, there goes my Christmas Day with Mr Arnold." She picked up Herbert and slipped him back under her T-shirt.

"Why don't you come round to us?" asked Lizzie. "Mum and I would love to see you."

"And I could bring your friends from Class Three around in the afternoon," said Jack.

Ms Wiz was staring out of the window, as if looking for Mr Arnold. "That would be lovely," she said quietly.

The Last Spell of Christmas

"A party for Ms Wiz this afternoon? All her friends from Class Three there?" said Podge's father Mr Harris on Christmas morning. "No way. Yuletide is a time for families, not weird, green-eyed women with magic powers."

"But, Dad," Podge pleaded. "Everyone's going to be there. For Class Three, Ms Wiz *is* family. Lizzie and Jack say she needs cheering up."

"She's always been trouble, Ms Who'sit," said Mr Harris. "What do you think, Mother?"

Mrs Harris placed a hand on Podge's shoulders. "I think that, if you don't let him go, you'll be cooking your own turkey," she said firmly.

"Typical," grumbled Mr Harris. "Not even Christmas is safe from that woman."

*

Ms Wiz sat at the head of Mrs Thompson's table, her pale face illuminated by the Christmas tree nearby. "This is the best Christmas I've ever had," she said quietly. "Before we have tea, I'd just like to thank Lizzie and Mrs Thompson for inviting me for Christmas dinner and to all my friends in Class Three for coming to tea."

She looked around the table at the smiling faces of Lizzie, Jack, Podge, Caroline, Katrina, Carl and Nabila. "Seeing you all again has reminded me of all the strange adventures we've had together."

"But we'll be having more adventures in the future, won't we, Ms Wiz?" asked Katrina.

Before Ms Wiz could answer, Mrs Thompson appeared at the doorway, carrying a large cake, which she put down carefully in the middle of the table. Written in green on the cake's white icing were the words, "HAPPY CHRISTMAS, MS WIZ."

"I don't know how to thank you," said
Ms Wiz.

"How about a trick?" suggested Jack.

"Yeah," the children agreed. "Trick!
Trick! Trick!" they chanted.

Ms Wiz held up her hands.

"I have an announcement to make," she
said when silence had returned to the
room. "After my recent . . . experiences
with a certain school inspector, I've decided
I want to lead a more normal life. Of course,

that . . . experience is over, but all the same I plan to get a flat somewhere around here. I'll be applying for a job as a teacher."

"Great," said Carl. "We can have magic every day."

"Well, no." Ms Wiz smiled. "The only way that I can become part of the normal world is to agree to give up magic."

There was a stunned silence.

"How exactly do you give up magic?" Nabila asked shyly. "Is there a strange ceremony with lots of Latin and chanting?"

Ms Wiz laughed. "All I have to do is—"

She was interrupted by the sound of three loud knocks coming from the hall.

Mrs Thompson frowned. "Who on earth could that be?" she said. There was silence as she walked out of the room to open the front door – followed by a blood-curdling scream.

The children stared at the sitting room door. First they saw a shadow, then a dark, cloaked figure filled the doorway, its fangs shining in the gloom.

"Yes." The voice coming from the figure was like ghostly wind rustling the leaves of an ancient oak tree. "I am Dracula." He moved slowly towards the table. "I have heard that the brotherhood of vampires has been mocked by one pretending to be the Lord of the Undead. Is this true?"

Nobody answered.

"Those who have laughed at the Undead

shall pay a terrible price," the stranger
continued.

"Is that you, M-M-Mr Arnold?" Lizzie
managed to say at last.

It was as if Dracula had heard nothing.
"First to pay—" the dark figure fixed
its eyes upon Ms Wiz, " — will be the
woman who actually danced with the
pretender."

Ms Wiz stood up slowly. "What do you
want of me?" she asked quietly.

"All I want—" Dracula sneered evilly as he moved more closely. "All I want—"

"Get some garlic from the kitchen, Mum," Lizzie said to Mrs Thompson. "We need to save Ms Wiz before it's too late."

"All I want . . . for Christmas is my two front teeth." With a pale hand, Dracula reached up to his mouth and removed his fangs. "Happy Christmas, Dolores," he said.

"Eh?" muttered Jack. "What's going on?"

Dracula took off his cloak, smiled, and put on a pair of glasses.

"I don't believe it," said Lizzie. "It was Mr Arnold all the time."

"A vampire for Christmas," said Ms Wiz, her eyes sparkling. "Just what I always wanted."

"Honestly," said Mrs Thompson. "Calls himself a school inspector and he comes round on Christmas Day to scare the living daylights out of children. This man's almost as odd as Ms Wiz."

"It's why we get on so well," said Ms Wiz.

"I just had to say I'm sorry about walking out of the Big Burger Bar," said Mr Arnold. "All those spells took me by surprise."

"Hey," said Caroline. "Now Mr Arnold's back, you won't have to give up your magic."

As if in reply, a faint humming sound filled the room. The lights lifted off the Christmas tree, hovered in the air, then made an archway over Ms Wiz.

"Listen to me, Class Three," she said, stretching her arms out in front of her. "On this Christmas Day, we are faced with a choice. If you wish me to live in your neighbourhood so that you can see me every day, I shall have to retire from being a paranormal operative. You have to decide whether you like me for my magic or for myself."

"For yourself," said the children.

"But the magic helps," muttered Jack.

Ms Wiz reached into her coloured canvas bag that was nearby. She took out Hecate, her enchanted china cat, and placed it on the table. "As from now, this is but a normal china cat," she said.

She reached into her T-shirt and took out her magic rat Herbert. She gave him to Jack.

"That," she said as Herbert ran up Jack's arm to perch on his shoulder, "is now but an ordinary pet rat."

"And I—" The humming noise faded. The lights returned slowly to the Christmas tree. "As from today, I'll just be Dolores Wisdom. Only in real emergencies will I become Ms Wiz again." She smiled, first at Mr Arnold, who stood beside her, and then at the children. "Any questions?"

There was silence.

"Just one," said Podge at last. "Are we
ever going to eat that Christmas cake?"

Laughing, Mrs Thompson passed Ms
Wiz a knife. Everyone clapped as she cut
the first slice.

"I say," a voice whispered in Jack's ear.
"I'd be most awfully grateful if you
slipped us a piece of that cake." It was
Herbert the rat.

"Er, Ms Wiz," said Jack quietly. "I think

the magic is still—"

Ms Wiz looked up and winked. "Still what, Jack?"

"Er, nothing, Dolores," said Jack.